Camilla Kuhn is a Norwegian children's book author and illustrator. She has a degree in graphic design from Central Saint Martins College of Art and Design in London and currently lives in Oslo with her husband, two children, two dogs, a cat, two guinea pigs, a tortoise, some fish, and seven walking stick insects. Visit her website at www.camillakuhn.no.

First published in the United States in 2016 by
Eerdmans Books for Young Readers,
an imprint of Wm. B. Eerdmans Publishing Co.
2140 Oak Industrial Dr. NE
Grand Rapids, Michigan 49505
P.O. Box 163, Cambridge CB3 9PU U.K.

www.eerdmans.com/youngreaders

Originally published in Norway in 2014 under the title
Samira og skjelettene
by Cappelen Damm AS
© 2014 Cappelen Damm AS
English language translation © 2016 Don Bartlett
All rights reserved

Manufactured at Tien Wah Press in Malaysia

22 21 20 19 18 17 16   9 8 7 6 5 4 3 2 1

ISBN 978-0-8028-5463-6

A catalog listing is available from the Library of Congress.

The illustrations were created using pencil drawings on
paper, digitally colored and enhanced.
The text type was set in Helvetica.

This translation is published with the support of NORLA, Norwegian Literature Abroad.

Samira
and the **Skeletons**

by Camilla Kuhn

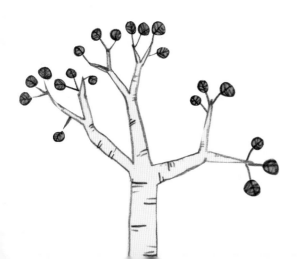

EERDMANS BOOKS FOR YOUNG READERS

GRAND RAPIDS, MICHIGAN • CAMBRIDGE, U.K.

Samira thinks it's wonderful being Samira! And it's wonderful being at school, and it's wonderful being best friends with Frida. But one day the teacher stands up and says something really horrible.

"Inside our bodies we each have a skeleton," the teacher says. "With a skull, and ribs, and a spine, and . . ."

"No way!" Samira shouts. "I do NOT! And neither does Frida!"

"Yes, you do!" the teacher says. "Everyone does. I have a skeleton, and Sven has one, and Serena, and Kenan . . . Everyone has a skeleton. Everyone in the whole wide world. You do too, Samira. And Frida," says the teacher.

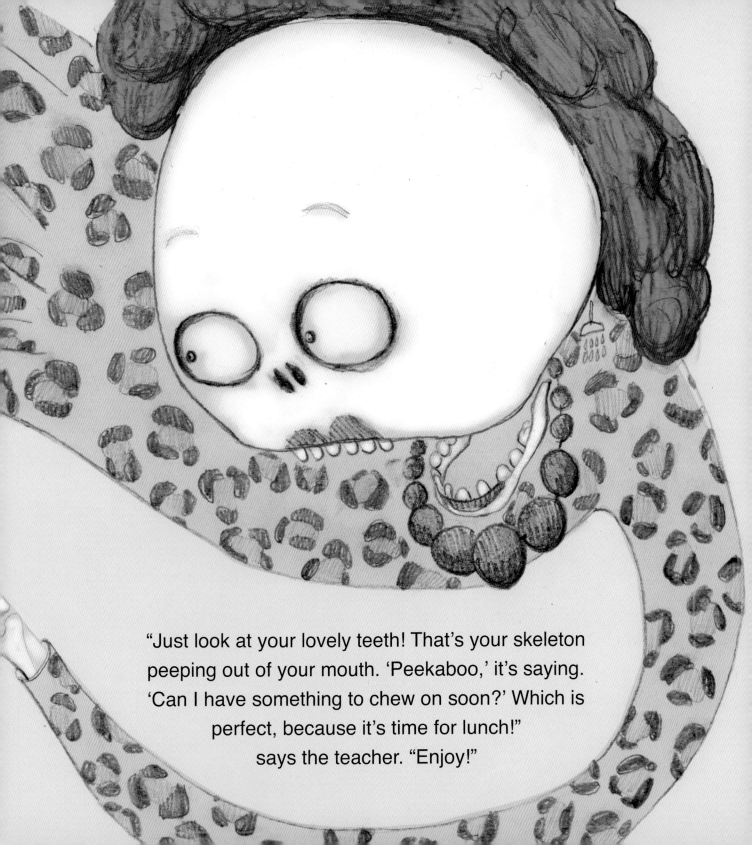

"Just look at your lovely teeth! That's your skeleton peeping out of your mouth. 'Peekaboo,' it's saying. 'Can I have something to chew on soon?' Which is perfect, because it's time for lunch!" says the teacher. "Enjoy!"

It's a terrible lunch break. It's impossible to eat with your mouth full of bones. And you can't talk either. "Want to sit together?" Frida asks, but Samira can't answer.

Frida and her skeleton sit somewhere else. *Fine*, Samira thinks, because she doesn't like Frida so much anymore. Skeleton-Frida.

Then it's gym class. The teacher shouts a lot. Run here, run there, jump and hop around and climb and do a somersault — with a body full of bones! Samira can feel them there and there and there. And the skeleton copies what she does ALL the time. "Now walk in pairs," the teacher says, and Skeleton-Frida comes over and wants to be her partner. But Samira doesn't want to be with HER!

Mom comes to pick Samira up. Bony fingers
and bony cheeks! She's not getting a hug. And
Samira walks behind her all the way home.

"Bad day today, Samira?" Mom asks.

"I have a skeleton," Samira says. "So does
Frida! And so do you! And so does everyone
in the world!"

"Is that so?" Mom says. "Yuck, how horrible!"
"I don't want one," Samira says.
"I can understand that," Mom says.
"Get rid of it!" Samira says.
"Okay!" Mom says.

"Can you do that?" Samira asks.

"Sure, I can," Mom says. "We'll just take the skeleton out and put it under your pillow, and then the tooth fairy will come and get it during the night."

"The tooth fairy?"

"Yes, and she'll be so, so happy! Imagine getting a whole skeleton when she usually only gets silly little teeth!"

Mom fetches some tools, a bucket, and some bandages, and Samira has to lie on the kitchen table.

"But don't I actually need a skeleton?" Samira asks.

"Not at all. Snails don't have a skeleton, and neither do worms, or jellyfish. And they manage just fine, don't they? Well, they mostly crawl around on the ground or float in the water, but that's just fine, isn't it?" Mom says.

"Yes . . ." says Samira.

"Here we go, then," Mom says. "Head or feet first?"

"Umm . . ." Samira says.

"I'll start with the head. Lie very still now.

One . . . two . . ."

The skeleton jumps off the table. "No, no, no!" it screams and runs out the door as fast as it can, down the road and all the way to the block where Frida lives.

Frida is sitting in the playground at the end of her street.

"Stop me!" Samira shouts. "It's my skeleton! It's gone completely nuts!"

"Mine too!" Frida shouts, and she starts hopping around and running, just like Samira.

"Hold me tight!" Samira shouts.

"And you hold me tight too!" Frida shouts. And they hold each other tight and laugh and dance. Then Samira says,

"And now my skeleton wants to jump rope!"

"Mine too," says Frida.

Samira and Frida jump rope in the yard.
The skeletons join in, but they can't be seen.
They're inside. Where they've always been.
Mom has packed away the tools.
That's good, Samira thinks.

Soon it is a new day at school.

". . . And under our skin we have muscles. They are the same as meat," the teacher says. "Exactly like a steak."

"*STEAK?*" Samira says.

"Yes, or ground beef. And you've got them too, Samira. And Frida. Everyone does. Everyone in the whole wide world," says the teacher.

"I still like you," Frida whispers to Samira.

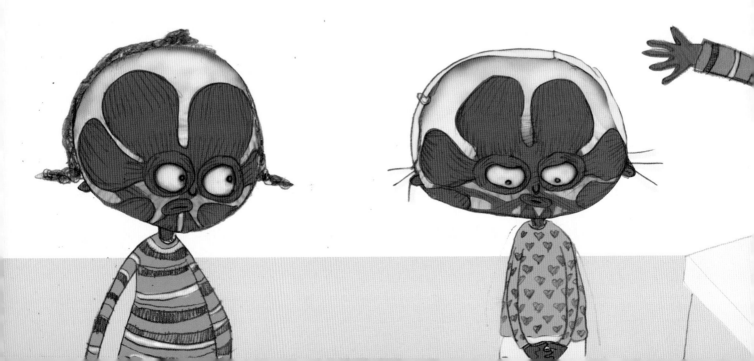

"And I like you," says Samira.